The Dark the Moon

by Jane A C West & Roger Hurn

Illustrated by Anthony Williams

Titles in Alien Detective Agency 2

Pirate Planet	Roger Hurn/Jane A C West
Spiders from the Stars	Roger Hurn/Jane A C West
Horror in the Chamber	Roger Hurn/Jane A C West
The Day of the Scoffalot	Roger Hurn/Jane A C West
Slime Time	Roger Hurn/Jane A C West
Take Two	Jane A C West/Roger Hurn
Jack and Wanda Ride Again	Jane A C West/Roger Hurn
The Dark Side of the Moon	Jane A C West/Roger Hurn
Fan Club	Jane A C West/Roger Hurn
The Onyxx Star	Jane A C West/Roger Hurn

Badger Publishing Limited
Oldmedow Road, Hardwick Industrial Estate,
King's Lynn PE30 4JJ
Telephone: 01438 791037
www.badgerlearning.co.uk

4 6 8 10 9 7 5 3

The Dark Side of the Moon ISBN 978-1-84926-932-2

First edition © 2012
This second edition © 2014

Text © Jane A C West/Roger Hurn 2012
Complete work © Badger Publishing Limited 2012

Publisher: Susan Ross
Senior Editor: Danny Pearson
Design: Julia King
Illustration: Anthony Williams

The Dark Side of the Moon

Contents

Vocabulary:

passport – a document that allows you to travel to other countries... or planets

antennas or antennae – feelers on the head of an insect / aerial on top of a TV

crater – saucer-shaped dent in the Moon where a meteor or asteroid has hit it

tremors – when the ground trembles before an earthquake

Main characters:

Jack Swift – the star of a top TV show

Wanda Darkstar – the Galactic Union's Alien Welfare Officer for Earth

Gorgonzola – Wanda's pet lunar mouse

STEALTH – Jack's spaceship, Space Tripping Extra Atomic Laser Time Hopper

Chapter 1
Passport to Earth

"That's odd," said Wanda.

"What, more odd than having aliens living on Earth?" muttered Jack to himself. Wanda didn't hear him, which was just as well – because she was one of the aliens who lived on Earth. She was Jack's partner in their Alien Detective Agency.

"All the mice on the moon are leaving," she said. "They've all applied for passports to Earth."

That was odd. Lunar mice liked living on the Moon. Jack looked at Wanda's pet lunar mouse Gorgonzola. He looked sad and his antennas were drooping. "Why are they leaving?" asked Jack.

"I don't know," said Wanda, "but we have to find out."

They jumped into STEALTH, Jack's spaceship, and hurtled into space.

The Moon was very quiet. Everywhere they looked, they saw empty mouse-holes. Not a tail, not a whisker, not a paw. They put on their space helmets and stepped outside.

Suddenly, Gorgonzola's nose twitched.

"What is it, Gorgie?" asked Wanda.

He squeaked loudly and scampered over to a small hole that was shaped like a door.

A little lunar mouse was hiding in the shadows. He shivered and shook, his whiskers trembled and his tail was tightly knotted.

"That's one rattled rodent," said Jack softly. "Don't worry! Spy Guy to the rescue!"

But to Jack's surprise, the little green mouse shook his fist – then scampered away.

"What's up with him?" asked Jack.

Wanda tried not to smile – but failed. "The mouse said, 'You're late!' And he wanted to know why the famous Spy Guy hasn't got rid of... the big, bad monster."

Jack gulped. "What monster?"

"Good question," said Wanda. Then the ground began to shake.

Chapter 2
Green cheese

"Earthquake!" yelled Jack. "Er... I mean, moonquake!"

"I think you mean RUN!" yelled Wanda.

Gorgonzola scampered into a nearby moon-crater. Jack and Wanda dived in after him. The walls quivered, Jack quaked. Wanda closed her eyes and pretended it wasn't happening.

Slowly the tremors died away. Gorgonzola opened one eye and squeaked at Wanda.

"He says that was the BBM," said Wanda.

"The what?" asked Jack.

"Big Bad Monster!" yelled Wanda. "Try to keep up, Jack."

Jack scowled. "If you're going to invent a code, you could at least tell me what it is," he said grumpily. "What does the BBM want?"

"Cheese, of course!" said Wanda.

"What do you mean?" asked Jack.

Wanda rolled her eyes. "Well, the Moon is made of cheese," she said.

"What?" said Jack. "No, it isn't: it's made of dust and dirt and rock."

"Oh really!" said Wanda. "Well, where do you think cheese comes from?"

"Cows!" said Jack. He knew the answer to that question.

Wanda looked at him in amazement.

"Don't have a brain attack, Jack! Cows eat grass – which is green. If cheese came from cows, it would be green, too. Duh!"

"Actually..." began Jack.

"That's why all the lunar mice have left," said Wanda. "The BBM is scaring them away from digging in the cheese mines. Whatever it is, it must be big."

"And bad..." said Jack, giving Wanda a cheesy grin.

Wanda wasn't laughing. "Lunar mice aren't scared of anything – well, not usually. I don't like the look of this."

Jack was going to say he didn't like the look of Wanda. But he did like having good looks and charm.

"I wish I could see what sort of alien this BBM is," said Jack.

The ground started to shake again.

"I wish you wouldn't say things like that, Jack," sighed Wanda.

"Why not?"

"Because your wish is about to come true."

Chapter 3
The BBM

Suddenly, a hole appeared in the wall of the crater. It got bigger... and bigger... and bigger... until... CRASH!

The whole wall fell down.

Staring out at Jack and Wanda was a HUGE, SCALY, ENORMOUS, LONG-TOOTHED, HAIRY... WORM!

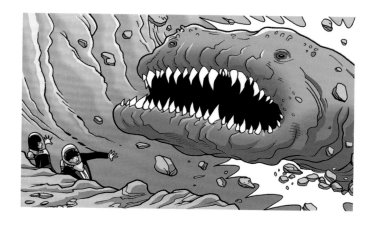

The worm's eyes glittered and it licked its lips.

"Cheesy!" it hissed.

"We're not cheesy!" said Jack.

"Only your jokes," whispered Wanda.

"Not funny!" hissed Jack.

"That's what I said," muttered Wanda.

"Cheesy!" hissed the worm again. And then he charged.

"RUN!" yelled Wanda, for the second time that day.

They climbed back out onto the surface of the Moon and hid behind STEALTH.

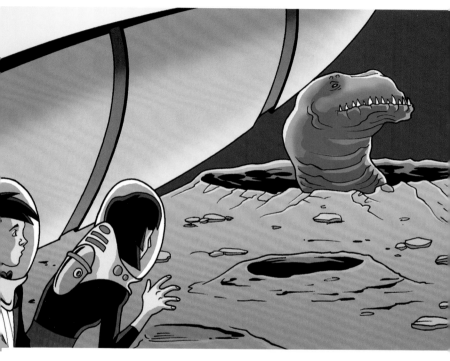

"How are we going to stop a BBM like that?" asked Jack.

Wanda shook her head. Her brain had already left the Moon.

Then Gorgonzola started squeaking and waving his paws.

"Hmm, that's not a bad plan," said Wanda.

"What?" asked Jack.

"It could work," said Wanda.

"What?" asked Jack.

"But it could be tricky," said Wanda.

"WHAT?!" asked Jack, shouting.

Wanda frowned. "There's no need to shout: Gorgonzola has a plan."

Chapter 4
Dark side of the Moon

Jack got out his torch. "It's really dark," he said.

"Duh! It's the dark side of the Moon," said Wanda.

Jack rolled his eyes.

"I know you're rolling your eyes at me!" hissed Wanda. "I can see in the dark!"

Jack sighed. Sometimes it was really hard having Wanda as his partner.

"Careful where you're walking, Jack," said Wanda. "The chocolate cheese mine is somewhere around here."

Suddenly she heard a loud thud.

"Ow!" said Jack. "I think I've found it."

His voice sounded a long way away. Wanda looked down at her feet. Jack was sitting at the bottom of a large hole. "What are you doing down there?" she asked.

"Looking for my fans," said Jack, joking.

"Stop digging for compliments and start digging," said Wanda. "We need that special chocolate-flavoured cheese."

"Urgh!" said Jack. "That sounds disgusting."

"Oh, it's very popular on Pluto," said Wanda. "But for some reason humans don't like chocolate-flavoured cheese. It's odd."

"Very," said Jack, to himself.

"The important thing is that the BBM won't be able to resist this special cheese. As soon as he smells it, he'll chase us."

Jack frowned. She said that as if it was a good thing.

He dug up a large piece of chocolate-flavoured cheese. Then he used his Spy Guy emergency rope trick to climb out of the hole.

"I really hope Gorgonzola's plan is going to work," he said.

"We're about to find out," said Wanda, as the ground began to shake. "Quick!"

They headed for STEALTH as fast as they could. It was tricky, because the Moon didn't have much gravity: every step sent them bouncing upwards. But the BBM was tunnelling through the cheese. And he was getting closer!

They made it to STEALTH just in time. The BBM's jaws shut just below Jack's favourite feet. "Time to blast off, STEALTHy!" yelled Jack.

The spaceship blasted up, up and away.

But sitting on the ground, carrying
a large piece of chocolate-flavoured
cheese – was Gorgonzola.

The BBM licked its lips – and charged.

Chapter 5
A lot of hot air

"This had better work!" said Wanda. She looked grim.

"Gorgonzola is a mouse on a mission," said Jack.

"Get ready STEALTHy," breathed Wanda.

Below them they could see Gorgonzola charging across the Moon's surface.

The little mouse was carrying the chocolate-covered cheese with his tail.

To the worm it looked as tasty as a sausage sandwich at a dogs' disco.

The huge worm was close behind, its teeth snapping at Gorgonzola.

The worm got closer and closer – and then it pounced...!

At the last second, Gorgonzola dived into a mouse-hole.

The worm went sailing over the top of him.

"Now!" yelled Jack.

STEALTH hit the worm with a blast of hot air from its engines. The worm shot up into space.

"Again!" yelled Jack.

Once more, STEALTH blasted the worm and sent it spinning off into space – spinning faster than a premier league striker's underpants in a washing machine.

"Goal!" yelled Jack.

STEALTH landed gently next to Gorgonzola. The little mouse looked very pleased with himself.

"Now it's safe for all the lunar mice to come home," said Wanda.

"What gave Gorgonzola the idea for the hot air?" asked Jack, curiously.

"Oh, it reminded him of you," said Wanda.

"Surely you're mouse-taken!" said Jack. "Geddit! Mouse-taken! Mistaken!"

Wanda sighed.

"Yeah, well, it's funny if you're me," said Jack.

"I've always thought you were funny," said Wanda.

Gorgonzola squeaked happily.

"He thinks you're funny, too," said Wanda.

Jack decided to change the subject. "I meant to ask," he said. "How come Gorgonzola doesn't want to live on the Moon with his friends?"

"Didn't I tell you?" said Wanda. "He's allergic to cheese."

Facts about the Moon

The Moon is Earth's satellite. This means it orbits, or travels around, Earth.

The Moon's gravity is 16.7% of Earth's. This means that a human who weighs 60 kilos on Earth would weigh only just over 10 kilos on the Moon.

The gravity of the Moon is the reason that the sea rises and falls with high tide and low tide.

Humans first landed on the Moon in 1969. The first man to walk on the Moon was American, Neil Armstrong.

The Moon isn't owned by any country on Earth.

Lots of countries in the world have myths about 'the man in the Moon' or the Moon being made of cheese.

The word 'lunatic' comes from the Latin word 'lunar' which means Moon. Some people thought the Moon could drive people mad. Myths say that people turn into werewolves when there's a full Moon.

Jack's joke

Q: Why do mice need oiling?

A: Because they squeak!

Questions

Why was Wanda worried about the lunar mice?

How did Wanda know that Gorgonzola was unhappy?

What did Wanda say the Moon was made of?

What did Jack think the Moon was made of?

Where does cheese come from?

What did they find on the dark side of the Moon?

Where was chocolate-flavoured cheese popular?

What did the BBM want?

How did Gorgonzola come up with his idea?

How did STEALTH help get rid of the BBM?